P9-APA-388

Pteranodon Soars

by Dawn Bentley
Illustrated by Karen Carr

To my husband, Raymond Jackson Harshbarger III, an amazing surgeon whose dedication and compassion have changed the lives of many children around the world—D.B.

To Todd Gauer with love—K.C.

Published by Soundprints Division of Trudy Corporation, Norwalk, Connecticut.

Book design: Marcin D. Pilchowski
Book layout: Bettina M. Wilhelm
Editor: Laura Gates Galvin

First Edition 2004
10 9 8 7 6 5 4 3 2 1
Printed in China

Acknowledgements:
Our very special thanks to Dr. Matthew T. Carrano of the Smithsonian Institution's National Museum of Natural History.
Soundprints would also like to thank Ellen Nanney and Katie Mann of the Smithsonian Institution for their help in the creation of this book.

Library of Congress Cataloging-in-Publication Data is on file with the publisher and the Library of Congress

A Note to the Reader: Throughout this story you will see words in *italic letters*. This is the proper scientific way to print the name of a specific dinosaur. In the story, "mosasaur" is not italicized because it refers to a family of dinosaurs instead of just one type of dinosaur.

Pteranodon Soars

by Dawn Bentley

Illustrated by Karen Carr

A *Pteranodon* shuffles toward the edge of a cliff. She hears the sound of waves crashing against the rocks below. She spreads her twenty-foot-long wings and jumps off the cliff and rises into the clear blue sky. She may not be very agile on land, but she is extremely graceful in the air.

Although *Pteranodon* is very large, she weighs only thirty pounds. Her bones are filled with air so she is light enough to fly. She soars on an air current, high into the sky.

Then *Pteranodon* swoops down to glide closer to the water. She is looking for something to eat. She relies on her huge, keen eyes to find prey.

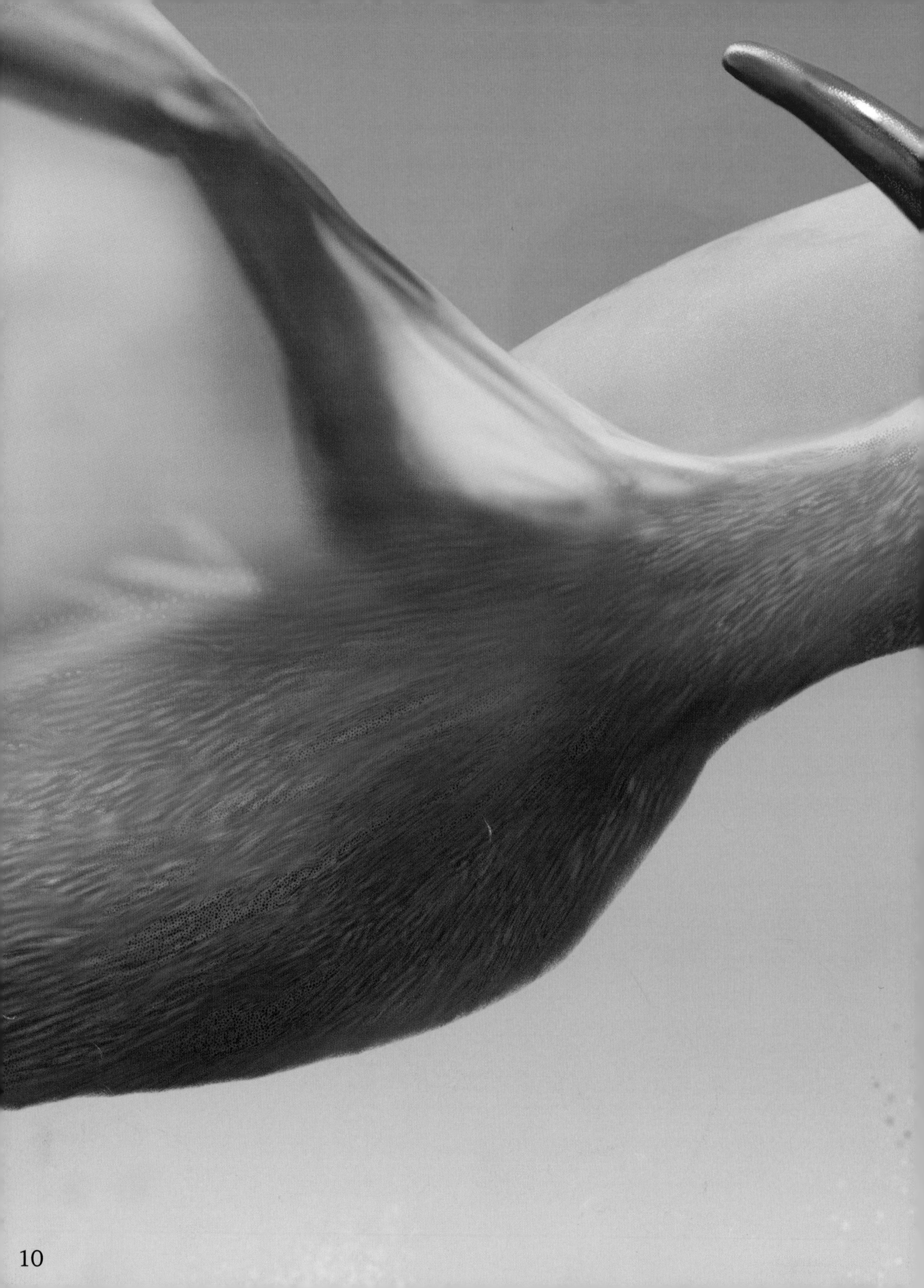

As *Pteranodon* glides over the surface of the water, she sees a school of fish. She dips her spear-like beak into the water and grabs several fish. She does not have teeth, so she swallows the fish whole.

Just as *Pteranodon* is about to pluck another fish from the water, she sees a huge mosasaur! *Pteranodon* is startled. Mosasaurs are her enemy.

She flaps her wings quickly and moves higher into the sky. With a splash, the mosasaur opens its huge jaws, but it cannot reach *Pteranodon*.

From the safety of the sky, *Pteranodon* keeps an eye on the mosasaur. *Pteranodon* is a strong flyer. She can stay in the air for a long time and fly long distances. Flapping her giant wings, she flies away quickly. Soon, the mosasaur is out of sight. *Pteranodon* hovers over several *Quetzalcoatlus* far below.

Pteranodon sees another school of fish. She dives down, dipping her long beak back into the water. This time *Pteranodon* does not swallow the fish. Instead, she stores them in her roomy mouth to bring back to her nest.

With her beak full of fish, she flies back up into the sky—even higher than before. She has flown far out over the water and now she must return to land.

When she reaches the cliff side, she sees a nest made of pine needles below. Pointing her beak and long neck toward the ground, she lands near the nest. The babies have just hatched from their eggs and they are hungry.

Pteranodon feeds the hatchlings the fish that she has brought back. Within minutes all the fish are gone, and *Pteranodon* is in the air to fish again.

The babies are small and helpless. They must rely on their mother to take care of them. When they get bigger, *Pteranodon* will teach them how to fly. When the babies are big enough, they will spread their long wings and soar through the skies hunting for themselves, just as their mother does now.

ABOUT THE PTERANODON (teh-RAN-uh-DON)

Pteranodon lived during the late Cretaceous period, which was more than 65 million years ago. *Pteranodon* were one of the largest flying reptiles of their time, but their bones were as thin as eggshells and filled with air, so they were very lightweight for their size.

Although *Pteranodon* had no teeth, their large brains and keen eyesight made them good hunters. They ate fish, insects, and small land animals.

One of the most recognizable features of *Pteranodon* was the large crest that stuck out from the back of their heads. Their heads could be as long as six feet! No one knows for sure what the crest was for. It may have helped *Pteranodon* keep balance in flight, or perhaps it helped to tell the males apart from the females, as the males had larger crests.

▲ **Mosasaur**

▲ ***Parasaurolophus***

▲ ***Quetzalcoatlus***

PICTORIAL GLOSSARY

▲ ***Pteranodon***